This book belongs to

_____

tate publishing
CHILDREN'S DIVISION

Felix
the
Wannabe
Firefly

Published by Tate Publishing & Enterprises, LLC
127 E. Trade Center Terrace | Mustang, Oklahoma 73064 USA
1.888.361.9473 | www.tatepublishing.com

Tate Publishing is committed to excellence in the publishing industry. The company reflects the philosophy established by the founders, based on Psalm 68:11,
"The Lord gave the word and great was the company of those who published it."

Book design copyright © 2013 by Tate Publishing, LLC. All rights reserved.
Cover design by Karla Durangparang
Interior design by Allen Jomoc Jr.
Illustrations by Greg White

Published in the United States of America

ISBN: 978-1-62024-770-9
1. Juvenile Fiction / Animals / Insects, Spiders, Etc.
2. Juvenile Fiction / Social Issues / Friendship
13.01.17

Felix the Wannabe Firefly is an inspiring story about the light that is in all of us, and when recognized and allowed to shine, illuminates not only our lives, but the lives of others. A heart-warming tale for all ages! A perfect gift.

—Denise Brennan-Nelson,
author of *Buzzy the Bumblebee* and *Willow*

With love, my husband John, and my three beautiful kids; Mariah, Olivia and JonPaul. And for all those who need a little more encouragement.

Don't forget: It's not how you start, it's how you finish. Don't give up!

Felix is a spunky little glowworm living with his beetle family in the roots beneath the Fane Forest. He has a gentle heart and the determination to be the best. But despite everything he is, there is one thing he is not—a firefly. And being a firefly is the single thing he longs for the most.

Night after night, Felix stares out his bedroom window and marvels at all the other fireflies as they flicker their green lights on and off. They look like little earthbound stars illuminating the forest as they dance in the darkness.

"Oh, I wish that were me," Felix sighed.

At that same moment an idea popped into Felix's head.

"I know what to do! I'll eat the same foods they do, and I'll *grow* into a firefly!"

Wasting no time at all, Felix headed for the swampy part of the forest. He cringed as he ate the slimy slugs and snails that were a regular part of the firefly diet.

He drank all of the Dancing Daisy's sweet nectar and—"*Achoo!*"—he sneezed away all the pollen before he could take a single bite. With a stuffy nose and a packed belly, he was so full he could hardly crawl back home.

When he finally arrived home, Felix decided he would attempt to fly and light up. He turned off the lights and crawled to the top of his bed. He closed his eyes and jumped.

"Ouch!" he said.

It didn't work. Felix had no wings and no light. Confused and upset, he crawled outside and watched in envy as the fireflies began to glow in the night.

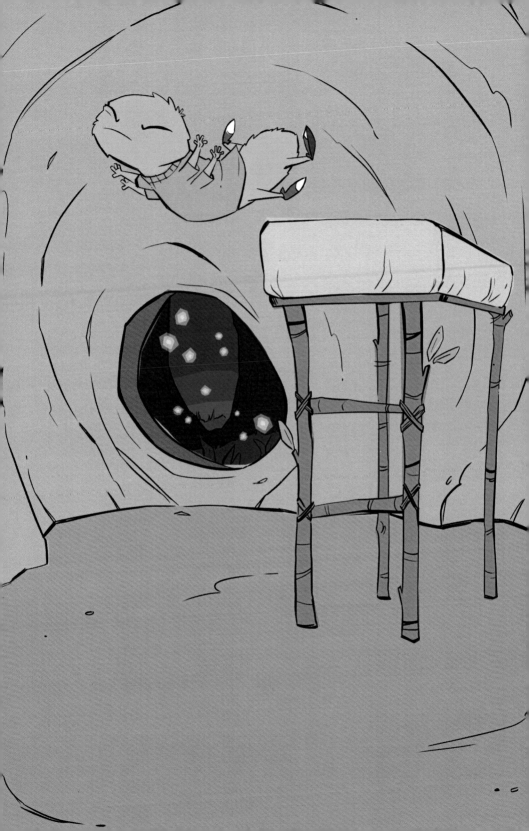

"Hey, Felix!" said a familiar voice. It was Sadie, the prettiest firefly in the forest.

"Hi, Sadie!" answered Felix.

"Do you want to play with us?" she asked.

"Yeah! Oh, but I can't fly," said Felix, embarrassed.

"That's okay," said Sadie. "We don't have to fly to have fun."

The two headed to the Laughing Lily field, where her other friends were playing hide-and-go-seek.

Felix was having so much fun he forgot about being a firefly altogether.

"Hey, Sadie!" said another familiar voice—Bruno, the biggest and most popular firefly in the forest.

"What are you doing playing with that little glowworm kid, Felix?" he sneered.

Then, Bruno and his friends surrounded Felix. Bruno's best friend, Charlie, pushed Felix on to the ground.

"Ouch!" said Felix. "What did you do that for?"

Bruno and his friends began laughing at Felix.

"Loser!"

"Haha you can't fly!"

They shouted and sneered until Felix couldn't hold his tears back any longer.

Then, Sadie pushed her way into the circle and grabbed Felix. "Let's go home," she said.

The next day, Felix and Sadie played together all day until the sun began to set in the sky. While Sadie's friends joined the firefly parade, she stayed grounded with Felix. Bruno and his friends flew by and shouted, "Felix can't fly!"

"Just ignore them," Sadie said. Felix smiled, trying to cover up the hurt he really felt.

Then, all of the sudden, the fireflies in the sky started to panic and fly in all different directions.

"Fly away!" someone cried.

"What's going on?" asked Felix nervously.

"Oh no!" said Sadie. "The neighborhood kids brought jars! We have to go, Felix!"

Sadie grabbed Felix by the hand and hid under a bush.

"I got one!" shouted one of the kids.

"Wow!" said another as they gathered around and stared into the jar. The kids filed out of the forest holding their prize up in the air.

In one of the jars, a firefly began frantically flickering his light on and off shouting, "Help! Please don't let them take me!"

Felix recognized the voice. It was Bruno.

"Oh no! They took Bruno!" yelled Charlie.

Felix and Sadie climbed out of their hiding place. "Someone should save him!" said Felix.

"Well, that's what he gets!" smirked Sadie.

"It's too dangerous," said Charlie.

"Yeah," they all agreed and walked away.

"Sadie, we can't just sit and do nothing," said Felix.

"Sure we can," said Sadie. "Let's just go home."

"Okay," said Felix, still bothered.

Felix could not fall asleep. He was worried about Bruno, and he couldn't take it anymore. He started his journey through the forest.

"Hey," someone whispered.

"Sadie?" asked Felix.

"Yeah, it's me. I knew you were going to try to save him," she said. "But you're going to need a little light."

Felix smiled. "Thanks, Sadie."

Sadie led Felix to the edge of the forest. "I can't go any farther."

"Okay. Thank you, Sadie," Felix replied.

How am I going to find him in all of these houses? thought Felix. Then a light caught his eye…Bruno!

He crawled over to the house and inched his way up to the window. When he reached the top he peeked in, and there he was. Felix crept through a crack in the window.

"Bruno, over here," Felix whispered.

Bruno stood up and looked around. "Felix?" he said. "What are you doing here?"

"I came to help you," said Felix.

"How?" asked Bruno.

Hmm, Felix thought. He scanned the room, and in the corner was a toy crane. He slid down the side of the windowsill, and raced to the crane. *Now how does this work?* he thought. Then he saw a big button that said "go." He pushed it with all his might, and the crane roared to life. Felix quickly looked to see if he had woken up the sleeping captor, but all he did was turn over in his bed. *Whew, that was close!* he thought. The crane began chugging forward, toward Bruno. He raised the crane and tried to grab the jar.

"Up just a little more," directed Bruno. "Got it!"

Just then the kid turned over and opened his eyes.

"Oh no you don't!" yelled the kid. He grabbed the jar with the crane still holding on to the top, the lid popped off, and Bruno took flight. The kid launched himself toward Bruno but missed. Bruno quickly scooped Felix up and sped out the window.

"Hooray!" they both shouted as Bruno flew home with Felix tucked under his arm.

When they arrived home, the forest was lit up with fireflies all in deep discussion to try and find Felix and Bruno.

"We're home!" they shouted.

"Are you okay?" their parents asked as they raced to greet them.

"We're fine," Felix and Bruno replied.

"What happened?" asked Felix's mom. Every firefly was quiet as Felix began telling his story. When he was finished the fireflies all cheered.

"Felix, why did you save me, when I was so mean to you?" Bruno asked.

Felix smiled. "Because it was the right thing to do."

Bruno gave Felix the biggest firefly hug he could give and said, "Thank you, Felix."

"I would like to award Felix the Fane Forest Light Award, the highest award in the forest," said the Mayor. "Because the light in your heart has shone brighter than any light I've ever seen!"

e|LIVE

listen|imagine|view|experience

AUDIO BOOK DOWNLOAD INCLUDED WITH THIS BOOK!

In your hands you hold a complete digital entertainment package. In addition to the paper version, you receive a free download of the audio version of this book. Simply use the code listed below when visiting our website. Once downloaded to your computer, you can listen to the book through your computer's speakers, burn it to an audio CD or save the file to your portable music device (such as Apple's popular iPod) and listen on the go!

How to get your free audio book digital download:

1. Visit www.tatepublishing.com and click on the e|LIVE logo on the home page.
2. Enter the following coupon code:
   fc45-936e-01fb-5ba1-66a2-893a-b278-4b36
3. Download the audio book from your e|LIVE digital locker and begin enjoying your new digital entertainment package today!